For Camille — E.J.

This edition published by Kids Can Press in 2017
Originally published in France under the title *Dans mes bras*.

Text and illustrations by Émile Jadoul
© 2016, l'école des loisirs, Paris
English translation © 2017 Kids Can Press

Kids Can Press gratefully acknowledges the financial support of the Government
of Ontario, through the Ontario Media Development Corporation.

Published in Canada and the U.S. by Kids Can Press Ltd.
25 Dockside Drive, Toronto, ON M5A 0B5

Kids Can Press is a Corus Entertainment Inc. company

www.kidscanpress.com

The artwork in this book was rendered in black pencil crayon and oils.
The text is set in ITC Stone Informal Std.

English edition edited by DoEun Kwon and Yvette Ghione

Printed and bound in Shenzhen, China, in 3/2017 through Asia Pacific Offset

CM 17 0 9 8 7 6 5 4 3 2 1

Library and Archives Canada Cataloguing in Publication

Jadoul, Émile, 1963– [Dans mes bras. English]
No room for baby! / written and illustrated by Émile Jadoul.

Translation of: Dans mes bras. ISBN 978-1-77138-841-2 (hardcover)

I. Title. II. Title: Dans mes bras. English.

PZ7.J25No 2017   j843'.914   C2016-907838-8

NO ROOM FOR BABY!

Émile Jadoul

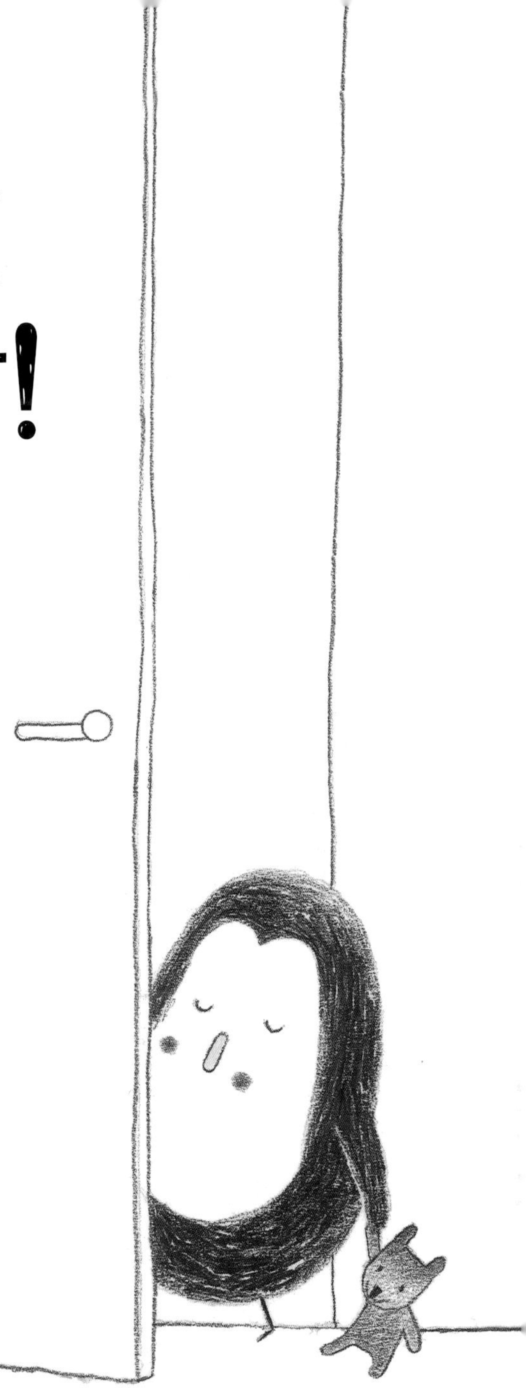

KIDS CAN PRESS

At last, Leon's little brother,
Marcel, has arrived!

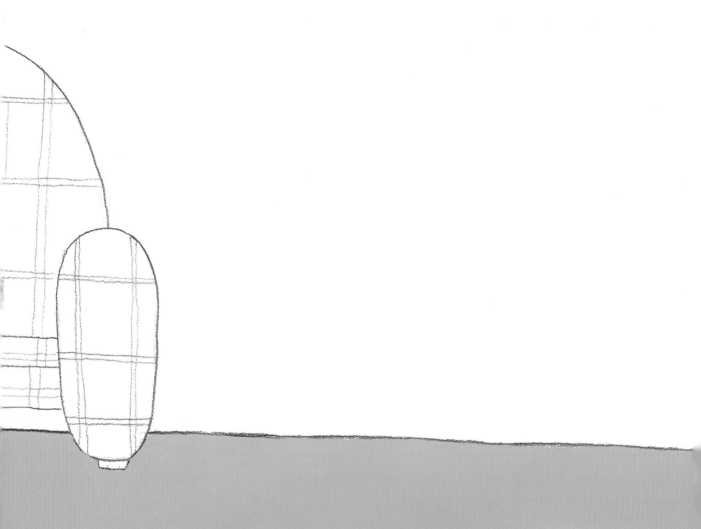

Marcel is sound asleep in his
cozy crib.

"He's going to stay in there forever,
right?" Leon asks.

"Well, not forever," Mama says with a smile. "He'll grow."

LEON

"Then where will we put him?"
Leon worries. "Not in *my* room!"

"And *not* on your lap. There's only room for me when we read a story."

"You know, Mama, your arms are way too big for a baby penguin. But they are just the right size to cuddle *me*," Leon says.

"And it's *way* too high up on Daddy's shoulders for a tiny baby penguin."

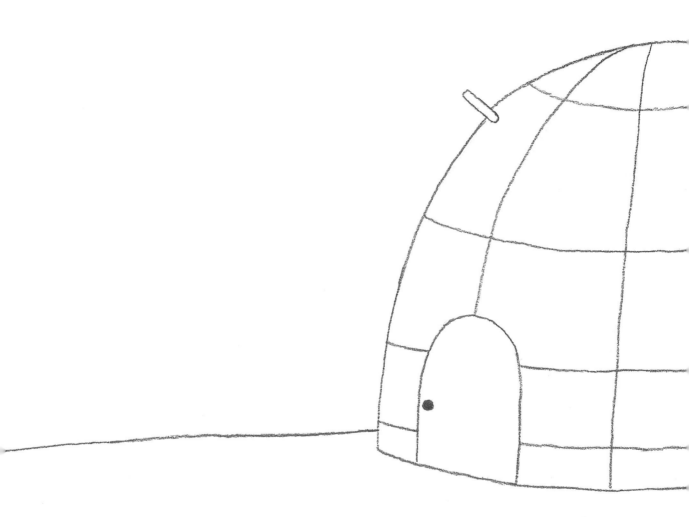

"*See!* Daddy on one side, Mama
on the other ...

… and me in the middle. There's no
room for anyone else!"

"We can't put a baby penguin
anywhere," Leon says.

And then, Marcel wakes up
with a little cry.

Leon thinks hard.

"I know where we can put
Marcel!" he says.

"In *my* arms ..."

"They are just the right size to
snuggle a baby penguin!"

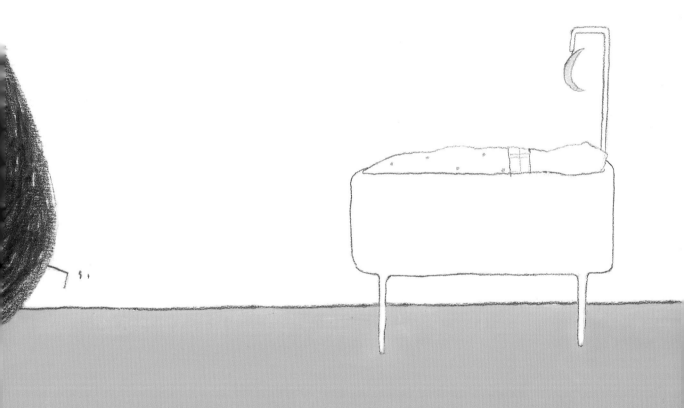

J PIC BOOK
Jadoul, Emile,
No room for baby!